Mama's Bayou

Bear hugs,
Dianne
de Las Casas ♥

Mama's Bayou

By Dianne de Las Casas
Illustrated by Holly Stone-Barker

PELICAN PUBLISHING COMPANY

GRETNA 2012

Copyright © 2010
By Dianne de Las Casas

Illustrations copyright © 2010
By Holly Stone-Barker
All rights reserved

First printing, February 2010
Second printing, September 2012

Library of Congress Cataloging-in-Publication Data

De las Casas, Dianne.
  Mama's bayou / Dianne de Las Casas ; illustrated by Holly Stone-Barker.
     p. cm.
  Summary: A mother rocks her child to sleep while listening to the sounds bayou creatures make at night.
  ISBN 978-1-58980-787-7 (alk. paper)
  [1. Stories in rhyme. 2. Bayous—Fiction. 3. Mother and child—Fiction. 4. Lullabies—Fiction.] I. Stone-Barker, Holly, ill. II. Title.
  PZ8.3.D3412Ma 2010
  [E]—dc22

                    2009042469

Printed in Malaysia
Published by Pelican Publishing Company, Inc.
1000 Burmaster Street, Gretna, Louisiana 70053

Chirp, chirp

Mama's by you on the bayou,
rocking you to the sounds of the crickets.
Chirp, chirp.

Mama's by you on the bayou,
rocking you to the sounds of the frogs.
Slurp, slurp.
Chirp, chirp.

Mama's by you on the bayou,
rocking you to the sounds of the snakes.
Sssss, sssss.
Slurp, slurp.
Chirp, chirp.

Mama's by you on the bayou,
rocking you to the sounds of the skeeters.
Zzzzz, zzzzz.
Sssss, sssss.
Slurp, slurp.
Chirp, chirp.

Mama's by you on the bayou,
rocking you to the sounds of the crawfish.
Clap, clap.
Zzzzz, zzzzz.
Sssss, sssss.
Slurp, slurp.
Chirp, chirp.

Mama's by you on the bayou,
rocking you to the sounds of the gators.
Snap, snap.
Clap, clap.
Zzzzz, zzzzz.
Sssss, sssss.
Slurp, slurp.
Chirp, chirp.

Snap,
snap

Mama's by you on the bayou,
rocking you to the sounds of the fishies.
Splish, splash.
Snap, snap.
Clap, clap.
Zzzzz, zzzzz.
Sssss, sssss.
Slurp, slurp.
Chirp, chirp.

Splish, splash

Clap,
clap

Sssss,
sssss

Splish,
splash

Chirp, chirp

Zzzzz, zzzzz

Slurp, slurp

Snap, snap

Big
bash

Mama's by you on the bayou,
rocking you to the sounds of the fiddle.
Big bash.
Splish, splash.
Snap, snap.
Clap, clap.
Zzzzz, zzzzz.
Sssss, sssss.
Slurp, slurp.
Chirp, chirp.

Mama's by you on the bayou,
rocking you to the sounds of her lullabayou.
Hush, hush.

Hush,
hush

Hush,
hush

Hush, hush

Hush,
hush

Hush,
hush

Hush,
hush

Hush,
hush

Bayou Wildlife

American alligator—A large reptile that lives in freshwater lakes, rivers, swamps, and marshes, mostly in Florida and Louisiana. It is the state reptile of Louisiana and Florida.

American green tree frog—A nocturnal amphibian that has suction disks on its fingers and toes. It is so unique in appearance that Kermit the Frog was modeled after it! The green tree frog is the state amphibian of Louisiana and Georgia.

Barred owl—Found in the bayous of the South, this is one of the few owls whose eyes are not yellow. People say its comical hoot sounds like, "Who cooks for me? Who cooks for you? Who cooks for y'all?"

Broad-banded water snake—A non-venomous snake that lives in swamps, *U*-shaped lakes, ponds, and slow streams.

Channel catfish—North America's most numerous catfish species. Catfish are named for the whiskerlike organs near their mouths.

Common snapping turtle—A large freshwater turtle with powerful jaws used to snap at a predator as a way of defending itself.

Crawfish—A freshwater crustacean also referred to as a crayfish, crawdad, or mudbug. They build tall "houses" out of mud and can swim backwards. It is the state crustacean of Louisiana.

Cricket—A nocturnal insect with long hind legs for jumping. The male cricket "sings" with a chirping noise when it rubs its two front wings together.

Dragonfly—A colorful insect with large eyes and two pairs of long, broad wings. It usually lives near an open body of water.

Fireflies—Also called lightning bugs, these beetles chemically produce a yellow, green, or pale red light in their lower abdomen. Many species are found in marshes or wet, wooded areas.

Great egret—A large white bird with long legs and an *S*-shaped neck. The egret is found in a variety of wetlands such as rivers, ponds, lakes, swamps, and marshes.

Louisiana black bear—One of sixteen subspecies of the American black bear, this bear is found mainly within the state of Louisiana. It is an omnivore, which means it eats both plants and animals.

Mosquito—A pesky insect of which there are 3,500 different kinds. The females bite the skin of humans and animals and suck their blood.

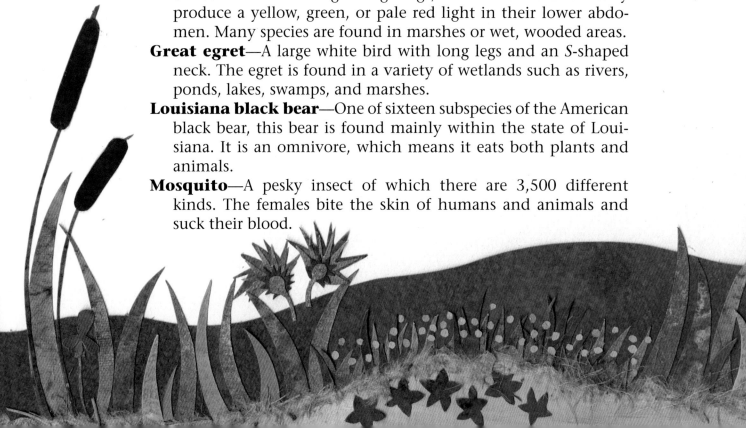

Bayou Vegetation

Alligator weed—A thick, green plant that grows in large mats on water and sometimes on shorelines.

Bald cypress—A tall, pyramid-shaped tree with needlelike leaves that are usually brown in the fall and dark green in the spring and summer. These trees thrive in the bayou because of the plentiful water source.

Cattails—Long wetland plants known for their spongy brown flowers and strong leaves. They are also commonly referred to as punks or corndog grass and are sometimes used as food or medicine.

Cypress knee—A structure in the root of a cypress tree that often juts out of the bayou waters. It helps to anchor the tree and provide it with oxygen.

Fragrant water lily—Native to North America, the lily known as *Nymphaea odorata* is one of the most easily recognized aquatic plants. Beautiful large white or sometimes pink flowers float on the bayou's surface surrounded by large, round green leaves also known as lily pads.

Giant blue iris—A light to deep blue wildflower typically found in freshwater marshes and swamps. The iris was named for the Greek goddess of the rainbow, because the flowers grow in many different colors.

Louisiana palmetto—Known as *Sabal Louisiana,* this palm has fan-shaped leaves and a stout trunk. Louisiana palmettos live in moist to wet soil and can be found from East Texas to the Florida panhandle.

Spanish moss—An air plant that uses trees and other plants for support.

Yellow-top—A leafy plant that bears bright yellow flowers in a fountainlike formation. Also called the early goldenrod, this wildflower, unlike other goldenrods, has no hair on its stems and leaves.

Author's Note

This story was inspired by the crickets chirping outside my window one night as I rocked my little girl to sleep. Living in Louisiana, I am awed by the beauty of the bayou and its lilting lullaby. Holly Stone-Barker and I worked together to depict the wonderful wildlife and vegetation that thrive in the bayou areas. Holly's medium of cut paper amazes me with its texture, depth, detail, and variety. Her specialty papers come from all over the world. I even had the privilege of shopping for paper with Holly in New York City! The next time you are surrounded by Mother Nature, stop and listen. You are sure to hear her sweet symphonic sounds!